TANNER TURBEYFILL
and the
MOON
ROCKS

ANNA BROWNING

ILLUSTRATED BY

JOSH CRAWFORD

DIAMOND DMT PUBLISHING

To my mom and dad, whose endless
support and unconditional love
got me to where I am today.
Thank you for letting me
chase my dreams.

A.B.

ISBN: 978-0-9837638-6-4

1. The Moon - Juvenile Fiction   2. Space Travel - Juvenile Fiction   3. Moon Facts - Juvenile Fiction
4. Rocks – Juvenile Fiction   5. Audio CD Narration - Juvenile Fiction   I. Crawford, Josh, ill.   II. Title

Library of Congress Cataloging-in-Publication Data   Library of Congress Number : 2013932235

Printed in the USA

First Edition   9 8 7 6 5 4 3 2 1

Disclaimer: This is a work of the imagination. All characters in this book are fictitious.
No resemblance to real persons, places or institutions are intended or should be inferred.

CD Production by StudioMVP/Mark Vincent Pence/Cedar Rapids, IA
www.studiomvp.com   mark@studiomvp.com

BOOK DESIGN BY JOSH CRAWFORD

ONE CRISP, SUNNY AFTERNOON, Tanner Turbeyfill
walked outside and across the yard to the tree house
he and his dad built last summer.

T HE TREE HOUSE was Tanner's favorite place to spend time because he had such a spectacular view of the sun during the day and the moon at night. Tanner's dad, Mr. Turbeyfill, was a retired astronaut. He had flown into space several times...

...but never to the moon.

TANNER DREAMED of going on his own explorations. He kept a moon journal, writing down every full moon and lunar eclipse he saw, because he hoped to travel to the moon one day. Tanner even wrote about what he thought the rocks were like on the moon. He had a large rock collection and he hoped to dig up some moon rocks to complete it.

SINCE TANNER NEEDED to wait until he was older to go to the moon, he decided to see if he could buy some moon rocks. So he walked down to Ridgewood, the town where he lived, to see if Mr. Rick's store had any for sale.

UNFORTUNATELY, moon rocks are very rare and there were none in the shop. Mr. Rick wanted to cheer Tanner up, so he pointed at a flyer hanging near the window.

Tonight there was going to be a blue moon! Every couple of years when there are two full moons in one month, a blue moon occurs.

Tanner was excited now!

TANNER KNEW the moon wouldn't really be blue, but he hurried home and climbed up to his Observatory to write about it in his journal.

He looked towards the moon through his telescope.

TANNER WROTE ABOUT
the craters he could see, how bright
they were, and how beautiful he
thought the moon looked on this
cloudless, starry night.

After a few minutes of observation,
the moon started to get brighter.
Tanner's eyes squinted as he tried to
figure out what was going on. He climbed
up the rope ladder to the tree house to
get a better look.

TANNER GAZED out the window when all of a sudden the moon turned a shade of royal blue and looked very mysterious!

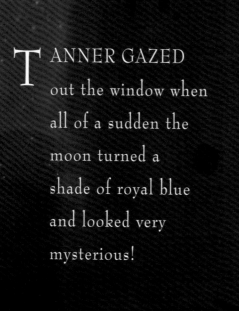

THEN A BRIGHT flash of light engulfed the tree house!

THE TREE HOUSE started to shake!
A tree limb whipped past Tanner's head,
transforming into a steering wheel.
Tanner shook with excitement!
He stumbled to the door and pushed it
closed, trying to block out the blue light.

When he turned toward the steering
wheel, he saw that a seat had appeared!
Tanner sat down and fastened his seat
belt. Not knowing what would happen
next, Tanner grabbed the steering wheel.

THE TREE HOUSE took off into the
sky. It had turned into a spaceship!
Tanner knew what he had to do...

...fly to the moon and dig up his own moon rocks.

Tanner turned his steering wheel toward the
blue moon, and the spaceship shot through the
Earth's atmosphere.

ONCE TANNER WAS FLYING
through space, he spotted something
up ahead. It seemed to be heading
straight towards him, growing larger...

and larger... and larger.

What could it be?

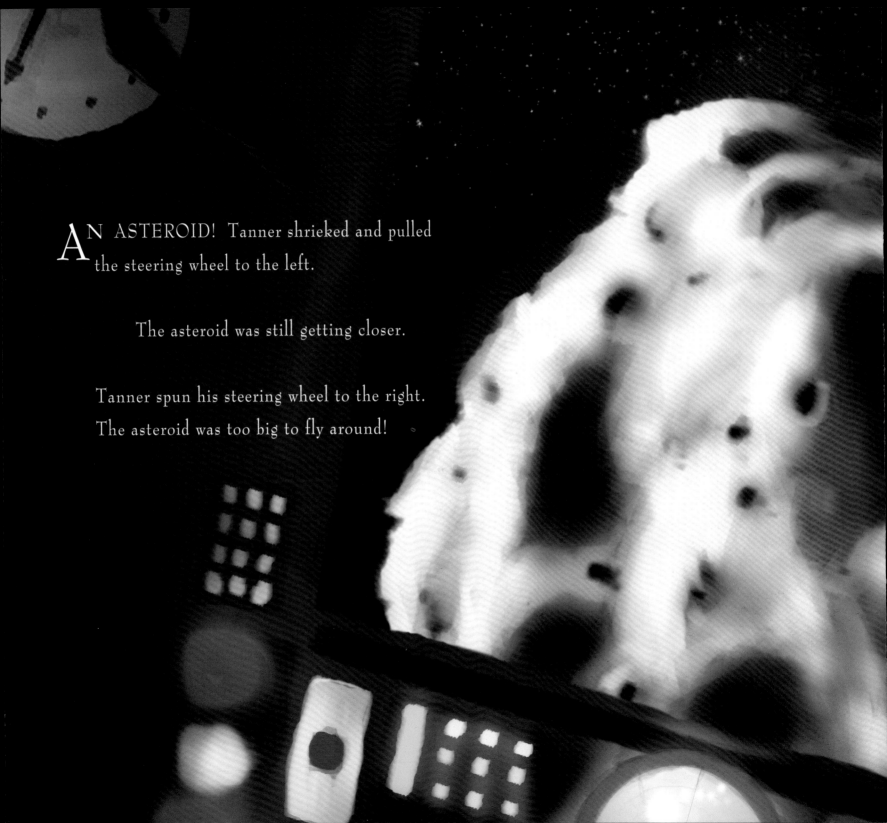

AN ASTEROID! Tanner shrieked and pulled
the steering wheel to the left.

The asteroid was still getting closer.

Tanner spun his steering wheel to the right.
The asteroid was too big to fly around!

Tanner jerked back on the steering wheel and flew
up and out of the asteroid's path just in time!
He sighed with relief as he turned the ship back
toward his destination.

WHEN HE FINALLY
reached the moon,
Tanner landed the
spaceship and got out.

He carefully investigated
the rough surface, walking
through deep craters and
jumping over sharp rocks.

TANNER WAS AMAZED
at all the different kinds of rocks he found.
Some were round and smooth. Some had
jagged edges. Others had holes in them
like Swiss cheese. Tanner put a few of
his favorite rocks in his pocket to keep.

AFTER AN HOUR OF EXPLORING,
Tanner noticed the moon was not as blue as before.

Was the brightness fading away?

Tanner started to worry because he didn't see the spaceship anywhere.

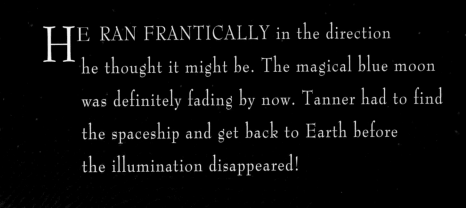

HE RAN FRANTICALLY in the direction he thought it might be. The magical blue moon was definitely fading by now. Tanner had to find the spaceship and get back to Earth before the illumination disappeared!

T ANNER WAS out of breath when he finally spotted the spaceship. He jumped in, buckled up, and blasted off toward Earth.

THE SPACESHIP LANDED in the
backyard just as the blue light vanished...
and Tanner's tree house was
back to normal.

TANNER WAS LIGHTHEADED
from the journey.

After writing about his trip to the moon in his
journal, he ran inside to tell his dad about the
adventure and to show him the moon rocks he
had finally collected.

AS HE EMPTIED HIS POCKETS, he told his dad everything that had happened because of the blue moon. His dad beamed with excitement and said, "Tanner, you're an astronaut now!" Tanner dashed upstairs with his moon rocks while Mr. and Mrs. Turbeyfill read through the moon journal.

IN HIS ROOM, Tanner added his new
treasures to his rock table, labeling them
"Moon Rocks."

His collection was now complete.

TANNER gazed out the window
toward his tree house and wondered
if anything could ever top his
magical trip to the moon.

SUN

JUPITER

URANUS

MERCURY

VENUS

EARTH

MOON

MARS

SATURN

NEPTUNE

GOD MADE TWO GREAT LIGHTS,

the greater light to rule over the day and the lesser

light to rule over the night. He made the stars also.

God placed the lights in the expanse of the sky to shine on the earth, to preside over the

day and the night, and to separate the light from the darkness. God saw that it was good.

(GENESIS 1: 16-18, NET)

TANNER'S MOON JOURNAL OF MOON FACTS

- The side that we can see from Earth is called the near side while the other side is called the far side.
- The USA's NASA Apollo 11 mission in 1969 was the first manned Moon landing.
- The first person to set foot on the Moon was Neil Armstrong.

The Moon is the only object in space that man has ever visited. One reason is that the Moon is much closer to Earth than the other planets (about 240,000 miles). The phases of the Moon are: New Moon, Crescent, First Quarter, Waxing Gibbous, Full Moon, Waning Gibbous, Last Quarter, Crescent, New Moon.

The Moon orbits the Earth every 27.3 days.

The Moon has a diameter of about 3,476 kilometers. It would take 130 days to travel to the moon by car.

The Moon can be seen clearly with your eyes, binoculars, or a telescope.

It takes 13 hours to travel there by rocket. At light speed, it takes 1.52 seconds!

Lunar atmosphere:

The Moon has almost no atmosphere, because of its weak gravity. Without atmosphere, there is no wind or water erosion. The astronauts' footprints remain unchanged on the Moon's surface and will last forever. The surface of the Moon features a large number of impact craters from comets and asteroids that have collided with the surface. Because the Moon has no atmosphere or weather these craters remain well preserved.

Temperatures on the moon:

The surface temperature fluctuates from +300F during the 2-week daytime to -270F during the 2-week night.

This is because there is not enough atmosphere to keep the Moon warm at night, or protect it from the Sun's rays in the day.

Lunar magnetic field:

The Moon has no magnetic field. You cannot use a compass to find your direction.

The moon causes many of the tides in the Earth's oceans. This is because of the gravity force between the Earth and Moon.

Moon Ingredients:

The moon is not made of cheese, even though it looks like Swiss Cheese. The moon, like the Earth, is made of ordinary rock. On average, there will be 41 months that have two Full Moons in every century, so you could say that once in a Blue Moon actually means once every two-and-a-half years.

Astronomy: a natural science that deals with the study of celestial objects (such as stars, planets, the moon, comets, and galaxies)

Astronaut: is a person trained by a human spaceflight program to command, pilot, or serve as a crew member of a spacecraft.

my DAD

ABOUT THE AUTHOR

ANNA BROWNING began writing in 2010 while working in a preschool classroom. She recognizes the extraordinary love that God has for children and this inspired her to write fun and whimsical picture books. She is a graduate of Western Carolina University and the University of North Carolina at Charlotte. *Tanner Turbeyfill and the Moon Rocks* is her first book. Anna loves coffee, books, music, going to the movies, and being involved in her church. She writes and lives in North Carolina with her fat cat, Leo.
www.anna-browning.com

ABOUT THE ILLUSTRATOR

JOSH CRAWFORD grew up in the mountains of North Carolina and received his education from Western Carolina University.
He lives in Waynesville with his wife, Amy and daughter, Alba.

www.joshcrawforddesign.com

TANNER'S TUNE – Let's Go To The Moon
Written & Produced by Mark Vincent Pence ©2013   Vocals by Dee Pittam

One night Tanner Turbeyfill
Leaned out of his windowsill
In his tree house with his telescope
He gazed above and dreamed and hoped…

Just like his dad, an astronaut
Tanner had but just one thought
To fly to the moon and out of sight
On a bright and beautiful, cloudless, starry night….

And now my friend as the moon turns blue
Imagine Tanner's trip is happening to YOU!
Hurry up…don't hesitate!
The moon is calling…don't be late!
Tonight's the night you take your flight.
Get ready to blast off! Hang on tight!

Rock-rock-rock in your Rocket Ship
Jump up high and get ready to flip
Over the asteroids as you dive and dip
Rock-rock-rock in your Rocket Ship

Now you're landing, "Oh, what a flight!"
Jumping around on the moon so bright
Filling your pockets to your heart's delight
With moon rocks and memories, "Oh, what a flight!"

But now the moon is fading fast
Your ship is almost ready to blast
Your cat is hoping that you'll be home soon
Time to say goodbye to the big blue moon.

Rock-rock-rock in your Rocket Ship
Jump up high and get ready to flip
Over the asteroids as you dive and dip
Rock-rock-rock in your Rocket Ship

But now the moon is fading fast
Your ship is almost ready to blast
Your cat is hoping that you'll be home soon
Time to say goodbye to the big blue moon.

Your heart is racing as you hit the ground
Landing back on earth so safe and sound
Then you hear Tanner whisper
"Oh, what a flight…"

On a bright and beautiful,
Cloudless, starry night…